Th
AM
of ABBY HAYES®

Now You See It, Now You Don't

ANNE MAZER

AN
APPLE
PAPERBACK

SCHOLASTIC INC.
New York Toronto London Auckland Sydney
Mexico City New Delhi Hong Kong Buenos Aires

For Kate Egan and Anica Rissi–
the fabulous Abby team

ISBN 0-439-68066-2

12 11 10 9 8 7 6 5 7 8 9 10/0

Printed in the U.S.A. 40
First printing, June 2005

Chapter 1

It has???

My Experience:

For the last couple of months, I've been helping out David, the director of the Jazz Tones band.

The Jazz Tones are a group of top-notch musicians at our school. They perform all over the city. One of my friends, Natalie, is a clarinetist in the band. Her friend Simon is the star saxophonist.

I am David's "assistant," his "right-hand," his "lifesaver," and his "best helper." These are all things that he's called me.

What I do is fetch the janitor, find extra music stands, collect checks for band shirts, and get diet sodas for David. I'm really an errand-runner.

David also calls me "Curly Red" (because of my curly red hair). I HATE that name. He has nicknames for all the other band members, too, like "Einstein" and "Flapper." He says he can't remember names otherwise. The only thing he does remember is music.

Aside from the nicknames, David is tough, but fair, as the band director. The Jazz Tones all like him. So do I.

What It's Taught (I Think):

1. It's hard work to direct a band.

2. It's also hard work to help a band director.

3. It's not always fun.

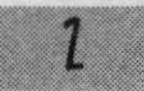

So why do I keep on doing it?

Because of Simon.

I've had a crush on Simon since the day I ran into him. Yes, I actually DID run into him; we almost crashed head-on in the hallway of Susan B. Anthony Middle School. That's where I first saw him.

Simon is a seventh-grader. He's one of the most talented kids in the school. He's a great musician, a great athlete, and a great student. Everyone in school admires him.

AND he's friendly and cute.

I run errands for David so that Simon will notice me.

<u>What I've Accomplished</u>:

1. Simon knows my name.
2. He says hello.
3. Sometimes we talk for five minutes.
4. I get invited to band parties at Simon's house.

Recently I got up the nerve to tell my best friend, Hannah, about my crush.

Hannah is always full of ideas. She had a plan for me.

She said I needed to do something more creative than running errands for the band director. She said I had to show Simon who I really was.

My favorite activity is writing. Hannah thought up lots of ways that I could use my writing talents for the band.

Hooray, Hannah!

Hannah's Brilliant Ideas:

1. Write bios for concert programs.

2. Design and post flyers for Jazz Tones concerts.

3. Interview David for school newspaper.

4. Do a profile on the musicians for school newspaper.

5. Spotlight Simon, the star saxophone player (heh-heh).

And What Happened to Those Brilliant Ideas...:

1. David has already asked the musicians to write their own bios for the programs.

2. David's girlfriend, a professional artist, is designing the posters and other materials.

3. I went to the newspaper to ask about writing a feature article on the Jazz Tones. The newspaper said I had to be on staff. They said if I joined now, NEXT YEAR I might write a feature article or interview.

4. They offered me an immediate assignment writing the Health News. It's a weekly update from the nurse's office, reporting on annual physicals, flu shots, and lice epidemics.

5. I said no, thank you.

What Else I've Learned from My Experience:

1. Brilliant ideas don't always work out.

2. To be creative in a jazz band, play an instrument.

3. To be creative on a school newspaper, join early.

Hannah told me that I should quit the Jazz Tones. She said I've done enough for them. She said that now it's time to do something for myself.

But I won't quit.

The Jazz Tones still need me.

And I get to hang around Simon every day after school. One of these days, he's going to really SEE me.

Mason stared at the desktop as if it were keeping secrets from him.

"Where's my pencil?" he demanded. "It was just here a minute ago."

"Maybe you put it away," Abby suggested, pushing a stray lock of her wild red hair away from her face. She put some papers in a folder and shoved it into her backpack.

It was Thursday after school. The final bell had just rung. Abby and Mason were getting ready to leave.

"I didn't," he said. "I put it right here. It's a very special pencil. It's the one that gets me A's on science quizzes."

"Do you have a *math* pencil that aces all your tests?" Abby asked. "If you do, I'll pay a month's allowance for it."

Mason smiled. The formerly chubby fifth-grader had become tall and slim in sixth grade. Now he was almost good-looking.

"Sorry," he said. "I only have a science pencil. But I'll help you with your math homework if you'd like."

"That's a full-time job!" Abby cried. "Math is my worst subject. Give me the alphabet over the times tables any day."

Writing was her best — and favorite — subject.

"Alphabets and times tables?" Abby's best friend, Hannah, joined them. "What are you talking about?"

Hannah was wearing an orange-and-pink striped T-shirt and jeans. Her long hair was in a ponytail. She was smiling, as usual.

"Mason's science pencil has disappeared," Abby told her.

"Disappeared? It must have run away. I *never* lose my science pencil," Mason said.

"Maybe someone stole it," Hannah suggested.

"If someone who always fails science suddenly gets an A, you'll know who did it," Abby joked.

Mason scowled. "Who would steal a pencil?"

"Can't you buy another one?" Hannah asked.

"This one was *special*," Mason insisted. "I can't replace it like a pair of worn-out socks. What could've happened to it?"

"Your pencil fell in love with a piece of chalk," Abby suggested. "They ran away together to a blackboard."

"Or the science pencil secretly wanted to be a history pencil," Hannah said.

"Ha-ha," Mason said. "You guys are really funny."

Natalie hurried past. She had a clarinet in one hand and a lime-green purse in the other. "See you at band rehearsal!" she said to Abby.

"The Jazz Tones *again*?" Hannah cried. "It seems like they rehearse every day of the week."

"We hardly ever get to see you anymore, Abby," Mason complained.

Abby shrugged. "The band has to practice. And I have to be there for them."

"No, you don't," Hannah said.

There was suddenly tension in the room.

"Yes, I do." Abby caught her best friend's eye. "You know why."

"Why?" Mason said.

Abby turned pink. "Never mind."

"You must have a crush on the director," Mason said loudly. "Aren't I right? It must be that ponytail and the foreign accent."

"No!" Abby cried. "I don't have a crush on David. And can you please NOT yell that to the entire school?"

Mason grinned.

Hannah picked up her backpack. "Let's go home, Mason. Since Abby's not going to walk with us. *Again.*"

She said it with a smile, to show that it was a joke, but Abby wasn't quite sure.

"I'd walk with you if I could," Abby said.

"You could walk with us if you quit the Jazz Tones," Hannah said.

"*You're* busy painting sets," Abby retorted.

"Not every day of the week!" Hannah said. "Not so much that I don't have time for my friends or other interests!"

Mason interrupted. "I've got to get going," he said. "Are you two going to stay and argue? Or are you coming with me?"

"*I'm* coming with you," Hannah said. She grabbed her backpack and followed him out the door.

Abby hurried after them. "Hannah!" she called. "Wait up!"

She needed to talk to Hannah and reassure her that the Jazz Tones rehearsals wouldn't last forever. "I'm still your friend, even if I'm busy."

Or did she really want Hannah to reassure *her*? Did she want her to say, "Don't worry, Abby, I'm not mad at you, I just have to tell you how I feel?"

Just then, Ms. Bean, the art teacher, stepped out of a classroom with a large box in her arms.

Ms. Bean was Abby's new favorite middle school teacher. She was young, enthusiastic, and full of ideas.

"Abby Hayes!" she cried. "You're just the person I was looking for."

Abby looked anxiously at her friends. They were already halfway down the hallway.

"Can you stop into the art room for a minute?" Ms. Bean continued. "I'll be there as soon as I leave this box in the office."

"Um, sure." Abby wondered why Ms. Bean

wanted to see her. She hoped that Hannah and Mason would wait for her.

"Hannah!" she called again. "Mason!"

Hannah and Mason turned and waved. Before Abby had a chance to say anything, they had vanished through the door.

Chapter 2

Worries of a Guilty Mind:

1. Whispering too much during art class today (Is that why Ms. Bean asked me to see her?)

2. Spending more time with the Jazz Tones than with my best friend

My Suspicion:

1. Ms. Bean, one of my favorite teachers, might ask me to be more considerate and quiet in class.

2. Hannah might be upset with me. Or am I upset with her?

Hannah understands why I have to attend all the Jazz Tones rehearsals. She knows about my crush on Simon. So why does she have to keep asking me to quit?

I don't know what to do anymore.

At least I know what to do about Ms. Bean. As soon as she comes into the art room, I'm going to apologize! I'll promise never to talk again during class. I'll be a model student.

Then at least one person won't be mad at me anymore.

"I'm sorry!" Abby blurted before Ms. Bean could say a word. "I won't do it again! I'm really sorry!"

Ms. Bean entered the classroom and shut the door. She looked confused. "What are you talking about, Abby?"

"I promise," Abby pledged, "*never* to talk again during class."

"That's fine," Ms. Bean said. "But it's okay if you talk, just as long as you don't disturb the students who are painting or drawing."

Ms. Bean perched on a desk. She was slim and petite. Today she was wearing overalls, a tie-dyed T-shirt, and green sneakers.

"Really?" Abby looked into the friendly eyes of her teacher and sighed with relief.

"Really," Ms. Bean said. "If you were talking too much in class, I would have spoken to you immediately. I called you here to share some good news."

"Does it involve Ms. Bunder?" Abby said.

Ms. Bunder was her fifth-grade creative writing teacher from Lancaster Elementary School. She was Abby's favorite teacher ever, *and* she was also good friends with Ms. Bean. They had coffee together all the time.

Abby loved it that her two favorite teachers were friends.

"Well . . ." Ms. Bean hesitated. "You *might* say so. She's definitely involved."

"She's going to teach here?" Abby said eagerly. That was her dream.

"No. I don't think she'll be teaching middle school writing classes anytime soon. She's hard at work on her novel."

Ms. Bean leaned forward. "You're going to like this, Abby. I'm planning to start a student literary magazine. Susan B. Anthony Middle School needs a forum for poetry, art, photography, and short stories. Don't you agree?"

"Yes!" Abby cried. She was already thinking of the essays and poems she could submit. "I do!"

"Ms. Johnson, the eighth-grade English teacher, and I are going to be faculty advisers. We're each selecting a few people to be on the staff. Would you like to be an editor?"

"An editor?" Abby repeated. What exactly did an editor *do*? Put in commas and correct bad spelling? "But I don't know how."

"Ms. Bunder thinks you'd be perfect. I do, too."

"Maybe," Abby said slowly. She didn't want to get stuck in another boring job — or one that she couldn't do. "When does it start?"

"We're meeting twice a week after school," Ms. Bean said. "Beginning next Tuesday."

"Tuesday?" Abby said. "I have a Jazz Tones rehearsal."

"You're a writer *and* a musician?"

"I'm not a musician," Abby said. "I'm just, well, I'm, um, the director's right-hand person."

"Right-hand person?"

"I, um, help out with the bookkeeping, and I, uh, find the janitor, and round up music stands, order T-shirts, and get sodas, and, you know, stuff like that. . . ." Abby didn't know why she suddenly felt so embarrassed.

"It sounds like a good experience," Ms. Bean said. "And I bet you're doing a great job. If I were the band director, I'd hate to lose you. But we *really* want you on the literary journal."

"You do??"

"*Yes!*" Ms. Bean said. "I hope we can tempt you away. We've invited the best writers, editors, and artists in Susan B. Anthony to join our staff. It's going to be a great group. You'll fit right in."

"I'm, um, really flattered," Abby stammered. "Thank you." Wasn't that what her mother said when she was invited to serve on a committee?

"And we want to publish your writing," Ms. Bean added. "Of course, you don't have to join the literary journal to submit work."

Abby's eyes lit up. "I have *lots* of poems and stories."

Ms. Bean smiled.

"But I'm not sure about being an editor," Abby

continued. "You know, the Jazz Tones . . . I mean, I'd probably have to quit."

"Take a few days to think about it," Ms. Bean said. "Let me know what you decide. I really hope you'll join us."

Chapter 3

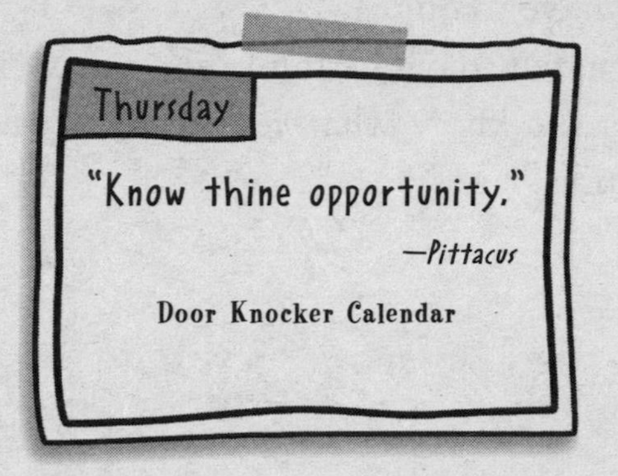

Mine Opportunity:

To join the literary magazine

To be an editor on the literary magazine

To publish my writing in the literary magazine

To work with the most talented writers, artists, and editors in the school

"This is a golden opportunity, Abby, and you'd be insane not to go for it." -Isabel Hayes, my older sister

Isabel said that it's a great honor to be chosen, and that I ought to be thrilled, excited, and grateful. She said that most sixth-graders don't get invited to be editors of anything.

(HOORAY! I've finally impressed my super-genius older sister!)

Isabel also explained what editors do. They choose the writing and art that gets published in magazines. It's a very important job. It also sounds like fun.

<u>Mine (Other) Opportunity</u>:

To work for the Jazz Tones

To be near Simon every day

To get to know him

I don't have any other opportunity to hang around Simon, my heartthrob.

Yes, my heart <u>does</u> throb when I'm around him. My breath stops, my eyes are dazzled, my lips tingle, and my feet dance. I've never felt anything like this in my life.

How do I choose between these two golden opportunities? It's almost impossible to pick one over the other. I feel very, very confused.

Help!!! What should I do?

<u>Announcing! A Hayes Book of World Records Poll</u>:

Abby Hayes, editor, writer, and publisher of the <u>Hayes Book of World Records</u>, has announced that she will poll friends, family, and acquaintances about her decision.

Should she join the literary magazine?

Should she give up the Jazz Tones?

Or can she work on the literary magazine AND be David's helper?

Abby Hayes will now go downstairs and mingle with mother, father, sisters Eva and Isabel, and brother, Alex. She will speak to friend Hannah on the phone.

(Friend Hannah is going away for the weekend! Sob!!! Must ask her advice before she vanishes!)

We will announce the results of this poll shortly.

LATER:

Extra! Extra! Bringing you an up-to-the-minute poll update!

Hayes Book of World Records Poll Results (sort of):

Abby Hayes, editor, writer, and publisher of the Hayes Book of World Records, has canceled her poll. She did not interview a single member of her family or any of her friends. This was due to . . .
um . . .

Um . . .

Never mind.

Abby Hayes, editor, writer, and . . .
oh, forget all that stuff, has canceled her poll until further notice because . . .

Because . . .

Well . . .

It's a bit embarrassing.

Why didn't I think of this before I announced my poll?

Abby Hayes has canceled her poll for now and forever.

The poll is useless.

She didn't bother asking anyone anything because she already <u>knows</u> what they'd say.

<u>What They Would Have Said</u>:

Hannah: Are you OUT OF YOUR MIND? Join the literary magazine!!!!!!!!

Eva: Ditto.

Isabel: Double double ditto.

Mother and Father: A choice between being an editor on a literary magazine and running errands? Do you even have to ask?

Alex: **DUH,** Abby!

<u>And a Few More Miscellaneous Responses</u>:

Ms. Bunder: Abby, I know you'd be a great editor. Go for it!

Ms. Bean: Don't throw this precious opportunity away.

Natalie: Give up the Jazz Tones? Why?

Simon: Good-bye.

Even though I have not actually spoken to anyone, I KNOW this is what they'd say. I mean, come on.

I will just have to figure this out without any outside help. (Does this mean I'm polling myself?)

Announcing . . .

ABBY'S SELF POLL

Reasons to Continue Working for the Jazz Tones:

1. Simon
2. Simon
3. Simon
4. Simon
5. Simon

(Repeat answers 1 to 5 until dizzy. Then rip up paper into tiny little shreds so that no one will ever read it.)

Reasons to Quit the Jazz Tones:

1. The literary magazine
2. To be published
3. To publish other people's writing
4. To work with the most talented writers and artists in the school
5. They really WANT me!!!

More Reasons to Quit:

1. More time for my friends
2. More time for writing
3. Hannah is right. The Jazz Tones job is going nowhere.
4. It's boring, too.
5. Actually, I don't like it.
6. I'm really sick of it.
7. I never want to fetch another soda for David!
8. Simon never notices me, anyway, so what am I doing there????

Wow.

I can't believe I wrote this.

I really DO want to join the literary magazine. And I REALLY want to quit the Jazz Tones. Even if a thousand Simons are playing a thousand saxophones.

My Self Poll worked. I got an answer on my own!!!

But now I'm scared.

What will David say?
What if I never see Simon again?
What if he forgets who I am?

Chapter 4

Friday

"If you board the wrong train, it is no use running along the corridor in the other direction."

—Dietrich Bonhoeffer

Lost Traveler Calendar

I think I got on the wrong train when I joined the Jazz Tones.

But now I'm going to get off as soon as I can.

Hooray!! I feel surprisingly light. Now all I have to do is tell David at rehearsal today. Will he be happy for me?

"Curly Red! Abby Hayes! There you are! Can you get someone to cut the lights in this place?"

David, the director of the Jazz Tones, looked harried. He ran his hand through his white hair and picked up a sheet of paper that had fallen on the floor.

The Jazz Tones were warming up in the auditorium. Abby glanced at Simon, who was blowing into the mouthpiece of his saxophone.

"Um, David . . ." Abby began.

"And then I need a soda from the machine," David continued. He rummaged in his pockets and pulled out some coins. "Diet ginger ale, you know which kind. If they don't have it, bring one of those lemon colas . . . or a bottle of water. But not the Sizzling Springs brand. There are trace metals in that water."

Abby took a deep breath. "David, I . . ."

"Rehearsal begins in five minutes sharp!" David announced to the band, then turned to Abby. "I'm glad you're here today. We have a lot to do."

"But I'm quitting," Abby blurted out, irritably. David didn't listen to anything unless it was a musical instrument. She was tired of trying to get his attention.

David raised his eyebrows. "Quitting?" he repeated.

"I'm going to be an editor on the literary magazine," Abby explained quickly. "Even though I'm only a sixth-grader."

He didn't look impressed. "Is something wrong?" he asked. "Are you unhappy here?"

Abby shook her head.

"You can work fewer days," he offered. "Maybe just twice a week?"

"I don't think so," Abby said. She'd made up her mind.

David frowned at her. "You made a commitment," he reminded her.

"But I need to break it," Abby said. "Working for the Jazz Tones isn't really me."

"You? This isn't about *you*. It's about the band."

"I'm sorry," Abby said miserably. What if he was right?

"Sorry?" David repeated in disbelief. "That's all you have to say?"

Abby gathered her courage. "I won't turn down the literary magazine. It's a golden opportunity."

There was a moment of silence, then David shrugged.

"All right then. Well. That's that." He turned toward the band again.

"Two minutes!" he called.

Tears filled Abby's eyes. Even if David wasn't happy with her decision, wasn't he at least going to thank her for what she had done for the Jazz Tones? Or wish her luck on the literary magazine?

For a moment, she wished she were back at Lancaster Elementary. It was a kinder place than middle school. Everyone cared about how you felt.

David hadn't even said good-bye. He hadn't said anything to the musicians. They were warming up their instruments as if nothing had changed. No one even glanced at her as she picked up her backpack and trudged out of the auditorium.

Not Simon, not Natalie.

Had she mattered that little?

Ten minutes later, Abby was in the schoolyard. She wasn't quite sure how she got there.

Tears blurred her eyes.

Everything was so confusing. She hadn't liked running around for sodas and sandwiches, but she still felt hurt by David's abrupt dismissal of her. Didn't she at least deserve a friendly good-bye?

"And then we went to the *best* club," said a familiar voice.

Abby sniffed and wiped her eyes. Brianna and Bethany were only a few feet away. Abby ducked behind a bush. She didn't want them to see that she had been crying. They had plunked down Brianna's white leather backpack on a bench and were searching through it.

Brianna was dressed in a turquoise miniskirt and a tiny lace top. She had a slim gold chain around one ankle. Her toenails were polished gold.

"And we had the *best* seats for the *best* show," Brianna continued as she rummaged in the backpack. "Where *is* that CD?"

"You didn't leave it at home?" Bethany asked. She was wearing jeans with daisies embroidered on the cuffs. Her blond hair was held back with daisy barrettes.

"I put it in the outside pocket right after I recited my poem in English today. Wasn't I *brilliant*? The '*Chanson* of Myself,' " Brianna sighed. "*Chanson* means 'song' in French. Remember, say it like this: '*sha-sone,*' " she pronounced. It sounded like she was pinching her nose.

Bethany clasped her hands. "Your *chanson* was so, so, so . . . neat," she told Brianna. She pronounced it "shan-sin."

"Neat?" Brianna snorted. "I'd call it extraordinary, spectacular, and astonishing."

"It was," Bethany breathed. She gazed at Brianna with shining eyes.

In fifth grade, the two of them had been best friends. Bethany had followed Brianna everywhere, a personal shadow. Then one day, she declared her independence. Bethany and Natalie became inseparable. She and Brianna weren't even friends anymore.

At least, that's what Abby had thought.

Now, as Bethany murmured encouragingly, Brianna began to empty her backpack onto the bench.

Abby watched as lipsticks, mirrors, face glitter, a hair dryer, a pink cell phone, the latest copy of *Me* magazine, a leather diary with BRIANNA'S MUSINGS stamped on the cover in gold letters, a pair of high-heeled sandals, a bright-yellow electronic organizer, and an MP3 player all emerged from its depths.

But no CD.

"Maybe you lent it to someone?" Bethany suggested. "Or lost it?"

Brianna tossed her dark hair over her shoulder and stamped her foot impatiently. "I'd *never* misplace or lose or lend out my Tiffany Crystal CD! I mean, it's signed by Tiffany herself. To *me*!"

"To you!" Bethany echoed.

Abby silently groaned. Was Bethany going to start chanting "Yay, Brianna," the way she used to?

Bethany began humming the tune to Tiffany's best-selling single, "Nasty Sugar Sweet."

"That's last year's hit," Brianna said irritably. "Haven't you heard the CD *Go, Girl, Gold*, and Tiffany's best-selling, chart-topping single, 'Eeuuuw'?"

"There's Abby!" Bethany chirped, noticing her for the first time. "Hi, Abby!"

"Hi," Abby said. She stepped out from the bushes, hoping that her face didn't give her away.

"Brianna was *finally* going to let me touch Tiffany's actual signature," Bethany said. "And now the CD is lost!"

"That's too bad." Abby tried to sound sympathetic.

"I'm so disappointed!" Bethany said.

Brianna replaced her things in the white leather backpack and slowly straightened up.

"Did you leave it in school or in your locker?" Abby asked her.

Brianna assumed her most tragic pose. "My Tiffany Crystal CD isn't lost, it's been *stolen*!"

Chapter 5

Lost, Stolen, or Strayed:

1. Brianna's signed Tiffany Crystal CD
2. Mason's famous science pencil
3. Bethany's little furry hamster key chain that's been on her backpack since third grade

In my opinion, the fewer Tiffany Crystal CDs in the world, the better. But Mason's science pencil is another matter altogether.

It's also sad about Bethany's hamster key chain. She said it was her lucky charm. She cried when she couldn't find it.

What do these missing items have in common?

1. All vanished mysteriously.
2. Their owners insist they weren't lent out or misplaced.
3. They're all "special" items.

Who is the thief? Why is he or she stealing pencils, key chains, and CDs? Why not money, jewelry, and CD players? Why bother with such small things?

Scary Thought:
My most "special" small item is my journal. What if someone steals it?

If someone stole my journal, it would be the worst, most unparalleled disaster in the history of the Hayes Book of World Records.

You can't read a pencil or a hamster key chain. There's nothing to read on a Tiffany Crystal CD, except how many trillions of copies have been sold, or how wonderful

Tiffany is and how much everyone loves her.

But if someone stole my journal, they would find out about my crush on Simon, how David treated me when I left the Jazz Tones, and how I feel about all my teachers and classmates.

That would be **TERRIBLE!**

I MUST KEEP MY JOURNAL SAFE!

Safety First: A Plan for Dangerous Times:

1. Drill hole in journal and chain it to my backpack.
2. Keep journal sewed into clothes.
3. Memorize entire journal and then burn it.
4. Digest journal. Tear into little pieces and chew slowly. (Yuk.)

I know! I'll put a fake journal in my backpack, with fake entries that anyone can read.

Even a thief.

Wow. School was so much fun today. We got all this, like, cool homework, and the teachers are the greatest. I just loved our math test. Then in gym, we were SO lucky. We got to do push-ups for a full half hour!!! Wish we had time to do even more. Next week we have folk dancing with the boys. Can't wait!

Hannah was away for the weekend, but now she's back. I'm dying for a chance to talk to my best friend!!!

Brianna was so quiet and sweet today. Her "Chanson of Myself" was so French. Bethany admired it a great deal. Mason's manners are outstanding. He ate his lunch without slurping once.

UGH! That was exhausting! The only true part was about Hannah. The rest was all false. My face muscles are aching from the phony smile I pasted on while writing it. My head is aching from trying to think of pleasant, nice things to say.

It's so much more relaxing to write what I really think.

Like, NO ONE BETTER STEAL THIS JOURNAL OR ELSE!!!

Warning!
Beware!
Forbidden!

If you open this journal without Abby Hayes's express written permission, watch out!

If you have read this much, you are already in deep trouble.

Close this book NOW!

Or the wrath of the Hayes will be upon you.

It was the end of the school day. Abby had just opened her locker and started to put away her books when Natalie rushed up to her.

"I can't *believe* you quit!!" Natalie scowled at her. "How could you?"

In elementary school, Natalie had been one of Abby's closest friends. They had done homework together, had acted in plays and gone to parties

together. Now, in middle school, their friendship had practically disappeared. Natalie had taken up the clarinet and started hanging out with musicians. She wore hip clothes, and acted bored a lot.

She and Abby had nothing in common anymore. Except the Jazz Tones.

"How *could* you?" Natalie repeated.

"Didn't David tell you that I'm going to be an *editor* on the literary magazine?" Abby said. "It's a great honor." She piled her books into the locker and slammed the door shut. "Our first meeting is in fifteen minutes."

Natalie didn't congratulate her. "David was in a pretty rotten mood on Friday after you left."

"I'm sorry," Abby said, although she didn't think it was her fault. "He wasn't too nice about my leaving."

"How can the band succeed if David has to worry about *details*?" Natalie cried. "I thought you were one of us."

"I *was*," Abby said. "But I didn't sign a contract for life."

"Oh, don't worry," Natalie said, changing her tone, "we're fine without you."

"Of course you are!" Abby retorted, stung by Natalie's sarcasm. She wished she had a more forceful reply. She knew she'd think of just the right words as soon as Natalie walked away.

"David interviewed a friend of Simon's," Natalie went on. "He thinks she's perfect. She knows all about music, too."

Abby's heart sank. Now some other girl would be the one hanging around the Jazz Tones and Simon every day after school.

If only Simon wasn't so heart-stoppingly cute! The way his hair fell in his face. His smile and his friendly manner . . .

If the new assistant was Simon's friend, maybe *she* was secretly in love with him. Who wouldn't be? Maybe Simon was in love with her, too, and that's why he had recommended her for the job.

Abby felt sick even thinking about it. She turned to Natalie. "Has Simon noticed that I'm not . . ." She stopped abruptly.

A group of girls had emerged from a nearby classroom. At their center was Brianna.

Everyone clustered around Brianna, who smiled at her subjects as if bestowing a regal favor. Bethany was gazing at her in adoration.

"My third cousin's wife's brother's uncle, the

famous jazz trumpeter, told me not to bother to audition for an amateur middle school kiddie jazz band. . . ." Brianna pronounced, with a quick side-ways glance at Natalie.

"Hooray, Brianna," Bethany cheered. She didn't seem to notice her former best friend, Natalie, a few feet away.

Once again, Bethany was a moth mesmerized by Brianna's light. She seemed to have forgotten all about Natalie.

Abby suddenly felt sorry for Natalie. "Are you okay?" she whispered.

Natalie shrugged.

"I'm performing at the City Theater this week-end," Brianna bragged. "I'm the youngest actress ever to have a starring role."

"You're the best, Brianna! Yay! Hooray!" Bethany's cry was ear-piercing.

"What happened to you and . . ." Abby's voice trailed off at the sight of Natalie's face. "Never mind," she said quickly.

Brianna and her admirers strutted down the hall in a cloud of shampoo-scented laughter.

Abby changed the subject. "Have you had any-thing disappear lately?"

"*What?*" Natalie said.

"You haven't been struck by the middle school bandit?" Abby kept her voice light. "A lot of our classmates are missing their favorite things."

"I haven't heard about it," Natalie snapped. "It doesn't sound too serious."

"It's serious to Mason and Brianna. Mason lost his science pencil. Brianna lost a Tiffany Crystal CD." Abby tactfully didn't bring up Bethany's name or her missing hamster key chain.

"Who'd miss a Tiffany Crystal CD?" Natalie said scornfully. "Her music stinks."

"Well, I agree," Abby admitted. "But Brianna is heartbroken."

"*Poor* Brianna!"

She shouldn't have even brought up Brianna's name, Abby thought. That was a big mistake.

"I hope it doesn't happen to anyone else," she concluded. Like me, she thought.

All day she had checked her backpack every five minutes to see if her journal was still there. She had tied it up with a cord and fastened it to the inside of her pack. No one could get it out without a struggle. Even her.

"I hope it *does* happen to someone else," Natalie

said. "We could use a little excitement around here."

"What if it's *you*?" Abby retorted. "Aren't you afraid of losing something?"

"My sanity," Natalie said sarcastically.

Abby sighed. Natalie was in a seriously bad mood.

Brianna could really get to you. . . .

"Don't worry, things will get better," Abby said, trying to console her. "I know they will."

Natalie looked at her. She seemed about to say something, but then changed her mind. She shrugged, picked up her clarinet, and walked away.

Chapter 6

If I read only the first sentence of a story or essay, will I be able to judge the whole piece? Will I be able to judge whether it's good enough for the literary journal?

I'll be the fastest editor in history!

Actually, I'll settle for really good – or good enough.

Can I please not be a terrible editor?????

I've just returned from the first meeting of The Daisy, our middle school's new literary journal.

The staff voted on the name. The boys wanted our literary journal to be called The Rat, but we girls outvoted them.

Thank goodness there are more girls than boys on the staff!

Would I have been as proud to be an editor on The Rat as I am on The Daisy? I don't think so!

Our Advisers:

Ms. Bean: twenty-something, patchwork jeans, yellow lace shirt, green sneakers

Ms. Johnson: forty-something, dark gray dress, pale gray stockings, gray suede loafers

Ms. Johnson is the eighth-grade English teacher. Kids say that she's a great teacher with extremely high standards.

I hope I can meet them.

What They Said to Us:

Ms. Bean: Your goal is to discover and encourage talent in your classmates and

give them a forum for their work. Let's inspire everyone to create new and exciting writing and art. The Daisy is going to be the best literary journal Susan B. Anthony has ever seen.

Ms. Johnson: It's the first literary journal Susan B. Anthony has ever seen.

Ms. Bean (laughing): Well, that should make our job a little easier!

Work of a Literary Journal: Or, What We'll Be Doing:

Art editors: Will choose photographs and artwork. Will do layout, journal design, and cover concept.

Literary editors: Will find readable, original, creative pieces for the magazine. Must balance fiction, nonfiction, poetry, and art. (We can't end up with twenty essays and one poem in an issue.) Will work with writers on revisions.

What if one of my friends submits a piece that I don't like?

What if I have to reject it? Help!!

Our Theme:

For this issue, the theme is "beginnings." Ms. Bean and Ms. Johnson picked it. In the future, the staff will choose the theme.

Our Staff:

The editor in chief is Katie, an eighth-grader. She seems really smart. There are two other editors, a boy named Lucas and ME! I am the only sixth-grader on staff!!

That really IS an honor.

The art editor is a girl named Amandine. She will choose the photographs and drawings, then give them to an eighth-grader named Matt, who will lay out the journal and format it on the computer so that it's ready for printing.

After we all got introduced to one another, the teachers gave Amandine and Katie a pile of art and writing submissions that they had collected.

We are going to advertise for more submissions. Our art editors will design a poster to put up in the hallways. Amandine proposed a large egg with a tiny crack to illustrate the idea of beginnings.

Everyone liked her idea. She will try to have the poster up by next week.

<u>What We Did for Our First Meeting</u>:

Made piles.

Everything went into three piles: poetry, fiction, and personal essay.

Then Katie went through the three main piles and subdivided into nine smaller piles.

She handed out piles to herself, me, and Lucas. Each of us ended up with three sets of submissions. She suggested that as we read them, we divide them into piles of "Yes," "No," and "Maybe."

Is this what it means to be an editor? Making PILES?

<u>A Question</u>:

(The very first question I dared to ask.)

What if we find our own work in the

pile? Do we have to judge our own submissions?

Help again! What do I do then?

Say, "This is the best poem or story I have ever seen in my life! It is brilliant beyond belief!"? (If I were Brianna, I'd definitely say that. But Abby Hayes never will. It's too conceited!)

A Staff Discussion:

"You shouldn't have to read your own work," Katie said. "If you get it by mistake, give it back to me."

"Anything I write is automatically in," Lucas joked. "Otherwise, what's the point of being on staff?"

"Ha-ha," I said.

Lucas has really curly hair that sticks out all over the place. He wears grimy glasses and faded T-shirts. He's a seventh-grader. I wonder if he knows Simon.

"There's no automatic acceptance, Lucas," Katie said.

Katie is very serious. When she talks to

you, she seems to look right into you. Her eyes are very brown and very intense.

"I'll make final decisions on staff submissions," Ms. Johnson told us. "That's what an adviser is for. This way none of you has to reject your fellow staff members."

"What? Rejection? Don't say that word!" Lucas cried. "No one is going to reject me, anyway. I'm a genius!"

Katie groaned.

I wonder if all geniuses wear such grimy glasses.

Ms. Johnson raised her eyebrows and said, "I can't wait until I get you in my class next year, Lucas."

Lucas grinned. "Me, neither."

I raised my hand. "What if you get a friend's piece? I mean, what if you have to reject your best friend?"

"That's part of an editor's job," Lucas said sternly.

I started to mumble an embarrassed excuse.

"Don't listen to him," Katie said to me. "That's what your editor in chief is for. If

you feel uncomfortable with a piece, give it to me."

"Thanks," I said. But I still felt nervous. The seventh- and eighth-graders are obviously tougher than me. Maybe I'm not suited to be an editor.

Will I even dare to submit my own writing to Lucas and Katie?

Even thinking about that makes me nervous. Katie is so smart and Lucas is so sarcastic. What if they rejected my writing? What if they laughed at it? Would I ever be able to face them again?

Back to The Daisy's First Meeting...:

On the other side of the room, Matt and Amandine pored over a pile of drawings.

Matt is very tall, with freckles and an irritating habit of cracking his knuckles. He wears shorts and sandals, even in cold weather. His legs are skinny.

(NOTE: Even if I didn't have a crush on Simon, I'd **never** have a crush on either Matt or Lucas.)

Amandine has wide cheekbones and almond-shaped eyes. She has perfect posture and a long neck. She looks like a dancer.

She and Matt were spreading out the pictures on the table and comparing them.

I wondered if any of Sophia's drawings were among them.

Sophia is one of my new friends in middle school. She is VERY shy. She's also one of the best artists I've ever seen.

End of Meeting:

We all came together again. We'll meet again on Thursday, and Amandine will show us a sketch for the poster. Then we'll go through more submissions, and maybe start to talk about the cover.

After End of Meeting:

Just as I was gathering my papers together and putting on my coat, Ms. Bean came up to me.

"I'm glad you're here, Abby," she said. "I can't wait to read your work."

"Um, yeah," I said. The thought of submitting my work to Lucas and Katie and Ms. Johnson made me feel kind of queasy.

"Find your best pieces," she instructed me. "See if anything fits in with our theme of beginnings. Bring them to the next meeting."

"I'm not sure I'll be ready," I mumbled.

"Don't worry," Ms. Bean said brightly. "We can wait!"

That wasn't exactly comforting.

Where I Am Now:

At home. In my purple room. Writing in my journal.

What I Need to Do:

Stop worrying about my own writing and start reading other people's writing.

Go through their essays, poems, and stories.

Divide them into piles of yes, no, and maybe.

What Else I Need to Do:

Call Hannah.

I haven't told her yet that I quit the Jazz Tones.

I haven't told her about the literary magazine, either.

She was out of town, but now she's back.

I can't wait to tell her the news.

Chapter 7

Wednesday

"What I tell *you* three times is true."

—*Lewis Carroll*

White Rabbit Calendar

I had to tell Hannah at least three times that I had quit the Jazz Tones.

She didn't believe me. She said, "I know you, Abby. You'll never leave as long as Simon is there."

"Well, you're wrong," I said. "I've left. Simon or no Simon."

Hannah shook her head. We were walking to school together. Usually Mason and Casey wait for us, but today they had to be at school early for a meeting.

"I tried my best to convince you and

failed," Hannah said dramatically. "Why would you leave now?"

"Because," I said with a touch of smugness, "Ms. Bean nominated me as the only sixth-grade editor on the new literary magazine, The Daisy."

Hannah stopped in the middle of the street. "This all happened in the last couple of days?"

"Yes," I said.

"So, are you also class president? Student of the year?"

"I'm just an editor on The Daisy," I told her. "And a former assistant to David. Ask Ms. Bean or Natalie."

"I don't believe you," Hannah said. "This is too good to be true. It's got to be an early April Fools' joke."

"It's not a joke. I really quit."

"No," Hannah said again.

"It's true," I said for the third time. "It's true, it's true, it's true."

Then we saw Simon.

He was a short distance ahead of us.

As usual, he was carrying his saxophone. As usual, his brown hair fell over his face in the most adorable way. As usual, he had the greatest laugh.

Next to him was a girl with long black braids. She was wearing wide red knee-length pants and high black lace-up boots.

I stared at her. Was she David's new assistant?

Hannah suddenly cried out, "Hey, Simon!"

"*Hannah!*" I protested under my breath. "You don't even know him!"

My best friend wasn't embarrassed at all. She asked Simon, "Is Abby still working for the Jazz Tones?"

Simon looked surprised. "No, she isn't."

Then he smiled.

I hoped that the smile meant that he wasn't mad like Natalie was. But what if it meant that he was *glad* I had quit?

The girl whispered something to him. He nodded and answered in a low voice, glancing in our direction.

I hope he wasn't talking about me. Or if

he was, it was something like, "Abby was the best assistant that the Jazz Tones ever had and David is heartbroken, blah, blah, blah . . ."

I hope that he wasn't saying, "She was our assistant, but thank goodness she left. You're SO much better."

Simon and the girl disappeared into a swarming group of kids.

Hannah was shaking her head and smiling. "You did it, Abby," she said. "You really, really did it."

"Yep," I said.

Hannah flung her arms around me. "Hooray, Abby!" she cheered.

Then Hannah and I talked about the thefts. Hannah hadn't heard about Bethany's or Brianna's missing items. Her eyes lit up when I told her.

"A real-life mystery!" she cried. "We can be detectives!!"

"Maybe," I said doubtfully.

"We'll use our powers of deduction, like Sherlock Holmes," Hannah announced.

I sighed. "Does this mean I'm supposed to be Watson?"

"Where's your sense of adventure, Abby?"

"Joining The Daisy is enough of an adventure for me," I said. "All I care about is not having my journal stolen."

And seeing Simon once in a while, I added silently. If possible, without any girls hanging around him.

Though I didn't say that to Hannah.

"We have to be on the lookout for clues," she said, ignoring my hesitation. "Together we can crack this case."

Now I think this journal entry is long enough. I'm going to stop writing. I'm going to put my journal back in its safe place in my backpack.

"Hi! Abby! Over here!" It was Sophia, Abby's new friend. She was waiting for Abby in front of the cafeteria. The two girls always had lunch together.

Sophia had long dark hair and long-lashed dark eyes. She wore embroidered jeans and a velvet shirt.

"Sophia! I can't wait to tell you about the first meeting of *The Daisy*. . . ." Abby began.

Sophia was a terrific artist. Abby wanted her to submit artwork to the literary journal and maybe even illustrate one of Abby's stories — if she got up the nerve.

But a dramatic shriek at the other end of the hallway interrupted her.

Startled, Sophia grabbed Abby's arm.

"My *Me* magazine!" cried Brianna. "It's missing! Kidnapped!!"

"Is that all? I thought someone had fainted," Sophia whispered. "Or died."

"Just wait. Brianna probably *will* faint," Abby answered. "With full orchestration and a cast of hundreds. Who'd want to steal a copy of *Me* magazine, anyway?"

"Not *me*," Mason said, joining them.

"Is that *your* favorite magazine, Mason?" Abby teased. "Brianna reads *Me*, but Mason prefers *Not Me*."

"The magazine of excuses," Mason joked. "For kids who get in trouble."

At the other end of the hallway, Brianna stamped her foot and demanded justice.

"I've gotta get close to *this*," Mason said. He plunged into the crowd rapidly gathering around Brianna.

Abby looked for Sophia, but she had disappeared into the lunchroom. For a moment she hesitated, then she followed Mason into the crowd.

"Are you sure you didn't misplace it?" a boy asked.

Brianna shot a thunderous glance in his direction. "I've already searched in my backpack six or seven times."

"That's right," Bethany echoed. "Six or seven times."

Brianna made a tragic gesture with her arms. "First my Tiffany Crystal CD and now *this*! Why do bad things happen to the *best* people?"

"You're the best, Brianna," Bethany chirped, right on cue.

A few feet away, Natalie was staring at her. A strange expression hovered around her lips.

"It must be so hard for Natalie," Abby whispered to Hannah, who had just appeared.

"Bethany is acting like a brainless Brianna babe," Hannah said. "I just don't get it."

"Why me?" Brianna moaned operatically. "Why *me*?"

"This is the best theater Brianna's ever done," Mason said, with satisfaction. "And we didn't even have to buy tickets. I'd like to shake the hand of the person who stole Brianna's magazine."

"But you lost your science pencil, Mason," Hannah reminded him. "You know how it feels."

"Yeah, I do," Mason agreed.

"And Bethany lost her hamster key chain," Abby added. "And now Brianna's *Me* magazine and her Tiffany CD."

Hannah frowned. "What kind of a person would want to steal all these things?"

"A me-first Tiffany fan with too many keys and a crush on Mason?" Abby suggested.

"No!!" Mason cried, clutching his heart. "Anything but that!"

Brianna shrieked again and swayed, as if she might keel over. Half a dozen girls rushed to her rescue.

"Nice touch," Mason said approvingly. "I like it."

Hannah stared off into the distance. "Has anyone noticed that the victims are all our fifth-grade classmates from Lancaster Elementary?"

Abby thought about it for a minute. "You're right," she said slowly.

"Is the thief someone from a rival class?" Hannah asked. "Or someone from another school whose team we've beaten in the past?"

Mason suddenly looked serious. "Do you think it's someone that we . . ." He didn't finish his thought.

The vice principal had appeared on the scene. "What's going on here?" she demanded.

Brianna made a rapid recovery. She wiped an imaginary tear from her eye. "My personal property has been unlawfully removed from my hand-sewn Italian leather backpack."

"You're not supposed to bring personal items to school," the vice principal observed. "The school can't be responsible."

"What?!" Brianna said indignantly. "That's all you have to say to me?"

"Everyone get back to your classrooms. Now," the vice principal ordered. "Unless you want a detention."

"It's a travesty!" Brianna cried. "A miscarriage of justice! I'll let my uncle's cousin's sister the judge know! Truth will be served!"

"With whipped cream and a cherry on top," said Mason.

"We *have* to pursue this," Hannah said to Abby, before she and Mason hurried to the next class. "There is a thief among us. He or she is targeting our classmates. Who will be next?"

Abby filled her lunch tray, went through the line, and slipped into the seat Sophia had saved for her.

"Whew," Abby said. "That was crazy."

Sophia grabbed the sketchbook that was always near her. "Nobody better touch my baby."

"That's how I feel about my journal," Abby said. She patted her backpack. Then she saw that the zipper to the main compartment was gaping open.

"Oh, no!" she whispered. Her heart pounding, Abby reached inside her pack.

The cords that held her journal in place were still there. So was her journal. Abby breathed a deep sigh of relief.

"My journal's okay."

"Check *everything*," Sophia ordered.

"I don't have CDs or magazines in my pack," Abby said. "Or lipstick or a cell phone." Her school-

books and papers were all jumbled together in their usual disorder.

"All present and accounted for," she announced. "Someone must have unzipped my pack while you were in line and I was watching Brianna. But they didn't get anything."

"That's good," Sophia said in a soft voice.

Abby knew Sophia was right. But it gave her a very strange feeling to think that the thief might have been hovering nearby.

Abby freed her journal and placed it next to her on the lunch table. "And now I'm going to write about it all."

She pushed a lock of stray hair out of her face. Something didn't feel quite right.

She reached into her backpack again. Her hand emerged empty. Then she pulled out her books and papers and searched some more.

"My earrings," Abby said in stunned disbelief. "They're gone."

She had taken them off before gym class and put them in her backpack. "They were the silver ones that my sister Eva gave me. They were really special."

Abby was having trouble breathing. She felt as if

someone had punched her. She had carried her backpack with her all day. She hadn't noticed anything unusual. No lurking strangers or unexplained accidents.

Was someone really targeting her fifth-grade classmates from Lancaster Elementary? Could it be someone from the other class or from another school? Or was it one of her former schoolmates?

Is it a person I know? she wondered. Somehow that thought made everything so much worse.

Chapter 8

Thursday

"It is more shameful to mistrust one's friends than to be deceived by them."

—La Rochefoucauld

Jelly Bean Calendar

I don't want to mistrust my friends! But one of them COULD have taken my silver earrings.

Who else would know how important they are to me?

Who else would know about Mason's science pencil and Bethany's beloved hamster key chain? Or Brianna's Tiffany Crystal CD and her Me magazine?

When I discovered that my earrings were missing, Sophia didn't meet my eye. She was suddenly busy sketching something.

For a moment I even suspected that Sophia was the thief.

But then I realized that she <u>couldn't</u> be. Sophia was only friends with ME, not Bethany, Mason, or Brianna. The person who stole knows us all very well.

I felt so ashamed of my thoughts, I could barely look at Sophia for the rest of the lunch period.

It's HORRIBLE to be suspicious of your friends. I'd rather trust them and be wrong.

But CAN I trust them? It seems like one of my friends <u>must</u> be the thief. Someone from another school wouldn't know us that well.

Or could they have made a lot of lucky guesses?

"Ha!" Lucas shouted. He ran his fingers through his already messy hair and threw a piece of paper across the table at Abby.

The librarian looked up from her desk and frowned at them. *"Ssshhh,"* she said.

Lucas only grinned.

With a sigh, Abby picked up the paper. "Is it good?"

"You'll see," Lucas said. He wiped his glasses on the edge of his T-shirt and grabbed another paper.

It was the end of the school day on Thursday. Ms. Johnson had sent Abby and Lucas to the library to read submissions for *The Daisy*. Katie had a doctor's appointment and had to miss the second meeting.

Abby wished that Katie were with them. Katie knew how to handle Lucas. Her serious manner would calm him right down.

Abby also didn't like sitting at a table with Lucas by herself. If one of her friends saw them, they might get the wrong idea. They might think she *wanted* to sit with Lucas and his grimy glasses, crazy hair, and loud shouts in the middle of the library.

And what if *Simon* saw them?

"So?" Lucas said. "What do you think?"

Abby started. She had been staring at the paper without seeing a word. "I don't know yet." She forced herself to focus.

"Cracked Linoleum" was the title. It was a sad poem about a boy and a floor.

"Um, it's a little strange, isn't it?" Abby said, when she had finished reading.

"Strange?" Lucas practically exploded. "It's *brilliant*!"

"Quiet!" the librarian warned again.

Lucas ignored her. "The cracked tile is a metaphor for life. Linoleum equals the despair of dailiness."

"*Huh?* I mean, yeah, of course," Abby said. "Whatever." She handed it back to Lucas. Katie had told them to make their own decisions. Lucas didn't need her approval. She wondered why he was asking her.

Lucas slapped the paper onto a pile. "In," he pronounced. "Most definitely *in*." He leaned back and put his feet up on a chair.

Abby sighed and shuffled her papers. She hoped that Katie and Ms. Johnson would veto "Cracked Linoleum." She hoped she didn't have poems like that in *her* batch.

She picked up a submission that had come in that morning.

"My Life," she read out loud.

"An all-purpose title," Lucas snickered.

Abby frowned at him. She wished he wasn't so opinionated. Or loud. Even though she agreed with him this time.

"My life has been a long, interesting one," the essay began. "I have had many interesting experiences, and have learned much wisdom. In my young years, I was blessed with an interesting family and many exciting obstacles to learn by . . ."

Abby threw the piece onto her reject pile.

"Another winner," Lucas said sarcastically.

"Maybe we should have a 'Bad Writing' issue," Abby said. If they were all like this, "Cracked Linoleum" *was* a work of genius.

Lucas grinned. "It might be hard to choose."

The next piece was a poem by an eighth-grade girl. It was called "Clouds Over Emerald Water."

It was stunning. It was absolutely brilliant. In spite of herself, Abby groaned. With submissions like this, she'd never *dare* to submit her work.

"Another bad one?" Lucas said.

Abby shrugged. She didn't want him to know how discouraged she felt, not only by the bad pieces, but by the good ones, too.

"Listen to this," Lucas said. "It's called 'I AM a

Star.' " He began to read out loud. "I am a star. The best, brightest, and most beautiful. At an early age, I began to show signs of extraordinary and brilliant talent in acting, modeling, dancing, horseback riding, and French."

"I know who wrote that," Abby interrupted. "Don't read another word. I've heard it *all.*"

"The big 'B,' " Lucas said. "The boastful, beautiful, bragging Brianna."

"How do *you* know her?" Abby asked in surprise.

"Can you keep a secret?" Lucas lowered his voice. "I take dancing classes with her."

"You do??" Abby gasped. She couldn't imagine Lucas dancing with Brianna. For that matter, she couldn't imagine Lucas dancing.

"Don't tell anyone," Lucas muttered.

Abby held up her hand as if swearing an oath. "I promise I won't."

Maybe there was more to Lucas than met the eye. Maybe he wasn't as awful as he seemed.

"How long have you been dancing?" Abby asked.

"Well, actually, since I was five."

"Seven years!" Abby cried. "That's practically your whole life."

"Tell me about it," Lucas groaned.

"If you don't like it, why keep on doing it?"

"I actually *do* like it," Lucas admitted, "but . . ."

He never finished his sentence.

One of Abby's former fifth-grade classmates chose that moment to burst dramatically into the library.

"Has anyone seen my electronic game player?" Zach asked in an agitated voice. "It's missing."

Zach and his best friend, Tyler, had been the computer geeks of the fifth grade. They carried their portable game players everywhere. They could recite cheat codes for every level of every game invented.

"You're not supposed to bring electronic game players to school," the librarian said.

"But have you found it?" Zach pleaded. "I've looked everywhere. It's gone!"

"No one left anything in the library today."

Zach glanced around the room as if he didn't quite believe her. Then he saw Abby. "Have you seen it, Abby?"

She shook her head. "I hate to say this, Zach, but it sounds like the Lancaster thief again."

"What?"

"Someone is stealing things from Lancaster Elementary kids," Abby explained. "Mason, Bethany,

Brianna, and I have all lost some favorite things. We don't know who took them or why."

"I better warn Tyler," Zach said slowly. "He has a personal organizer with everything on it. If it was stolen, he'd be lost."

"Good idea," Abby said. "And I'm sorry about your electronic game player. Maybe it'll turn up."

"Maybe." Zach sounded depressed. "I mowed lawns all summer to buy it. It's going to take me *months* to get another one." He stumbled out of the library.

"Thief?" Lucas's eyes were bright. "What's this?"

"You heard it," Abby said.

"Maybe I can write a whodunit," Lucas said eagerly. "You know, like 'in the somber halls of the middle school, an unknown thief prowled stealthily, his agile hands slipping in and out of carefully unzipped backpacks . . .' "

Abby looked away in annoyance. How could Lucas think of writing a story at a time like this? If she had thought that she had liked him for a moment, that moment was gone.

Chapter 9

Saturday

"Sometimes I have believed as many as six impossible things before breakfast."

—*Lewis Carroll*

Conundrum Calendar

<u>Six Impossible Things I Have Believed Before Breakfast</u>:

(Well, actually, it was <u>after</u> breakfast, but never mind . . .)

1. The thief is not going to steal any-more.

Wrong. Hannah came over this morning to tell me that one of her hand-beaded bracelets was stolen yesterday. It was orange and turquoise and yellow, her favorite colors. Hannah made it herself.

2. Hannah is too cheerful and happy to let a stolen bracelet bother her. And besides, she can make as many bracelets as she wants.

Wrong. Hannah is VERY upset. She is even more upset than I am about my silver earrings.

"Why?" she kept saying over and over. "Why? I never did anything to anyone."

3. I can always cheer Hannah up.

Wrong.

"My silver earrings were innocent, too," I said, trying to make a joke. "They never did anything to anyone, either."

Hannah didn't even smile.

4. Once Hannah realizes how clever this thief is, she'll give up the crazy idea of solving the mystery.

Really wrong. Now Hannah is more determined than ever to find the thief.

"We have to find out who it is," she said.

"But how?" I asked.

"By finding out why," she answered firmly.

"But how?" I said again.

"We'll need to know who," she answered.

5. Hannah will always listen to reason.

Really, really wrong.

"We're in over our heads here. Let's go to one of our teachers. Or the principal," I said.

"Do you think they care?" Hannah retorted. "They'll just give us that line about not bringing personal items to school. You heard the vice principal."

"This is a tough situation," I insisted. "It's too much for the two of us. We need an adult."

"We can do it, Abby," Hannah insisted right back. "You and I can understand a kid's mind better than any adult."

6. I will simply tell Hannah that I don't want to be involved.

Wrong, wrong, WRONG!

"I can't," I said. "I have too many things on my mind."

"Like what? Simon?" Hannah said.

I didn't answer.

"You're my best friend!" Hannah pleaded. "Besides, you don't have to do anything. Just hang around and help me with a few ideas."

"I think we should go to the guidance office about this."

"If we don't get anywhere in a week, I'll make the appointment myself," Hannah promised. "Will you help me until then? Please, Abby! Please! I've always wanted to solve a mystery."

"Oh, all right, I guess," I conceded.

Hannah smiled for the first time that morning.

Then we started brainstorming.

"Let's face the facts," Hannah said. "One of our friends or classmates has got to be doing this because they know exactly what to take. That narrows it down to about fifty potential suspects, probably from either Ms. Kantor's or Mrs. McMillan's fifth-grade class."

"Just a few suspects," I said, a bit sarcastically.

Both of us were silent for a moment.

Six Possible Plans That Hannah and I Thought up on a Saturday Morning:

1. Put all former Lancaster Elementary students on red alert.

2. Do a survey. Find out who's missing things and who isn't.

3. Interview victims. Find out exactly where they were, what they were doing, and when they discovered their loss.

4. Interview all Lancaster students who HAVEN'T lost anything.

5. Look for suspicious patterns.

6. Set a trap for the thief.

We decided to interview ourselves first.

Hannah's Interview with Me:

Hannah: Did you notice anything suspicious when your earrings disappeared?

Me: No.

Hannah: Any unusual characters lurking about?

Me: No.

Hannah: Who was there?

Me: Sophia, you, and Mason. And a lot of other kids.

Hannah: What were you doing between the last time you saw your earrings and the moment they disappeared?

Me: I took them off before gym, put them in my backpack, locked them in my locker, and then forgot to put them back on after gym. They were in my backpack while I went to my classes.

Hannah: Is there any reason why someone would steal your earrings?

Me: No.

My Interview with Hannah:

More or less the same. Except she took

off her bracelet in art class so she wouldn't get paint on it.

Then we made a list of all former Lancaster Elementary students who HAVEN'T had something stolen.

1. Casey. Mason's best friend and one of our best friends! It CAN'T be Casey!!!

2. Natalie. One of our former best friends. Aside from being too busy to steal, Natalie'd NEVER do anything like this!!

3. Victoria. Brianna's friend and the meanest girl in school. Is she having a fight with Brianna? Is that why Brianna has had two items stolen?

No, Victoria would never steal a hamster key chain, a science pencil, or a *Me* magazine. She'd steal people's diaries and journals to learn their secrets; then she'd torment and blackmail them.

4. Tyler. Zach's best friend. Has own electronic game machine, why would he take Zach's? Not likely.

5. Jonathan. Former classmate. Would

never notice anyone's favorite items, much less steal them.

6. Crystal. Wears tight skirts, skimpy tops, and loads of makeup. The only thing she'd steal is someone's boyfriend.

7. Jessica. My former best friend. In Oregon. Too far away. Can't steal.

We also made a list of all former Lancaster Elementary students who HAVE had something stolen.

Maybe the thief has stolen his or her own possessions just to confuse everyone? (It doesn't really make sense, but as Hannah said, we have to think of everything.)

1. Mason. *No, no, no, no, NO!* It's not Mason!

2. Brianna. Will do ANYTHING for attention. But steal?

3. Bethany. Secretly angry at Brianna? But she was crying over her lost hamster key chain. And she's not an actress like Brianna.

4. Abby. Who, me? *No way!!!*

5. Zach. Too busy playing electronic games to steal.

6. Hannah. Too friendly, outgoing, and honest. Can't even comprehend how anyone would WANT to steal.

<u>Six Probable Problems That Hannah and I Identified</u>:

1. The thief is very skillful. No one notices him or her.

2. We have no idea why he or she is doing this.

3. We don't know where she or he will strike next.

4. One thing's for sure, we probably know the person.

5. Do we really want to uncover his or her identity?

6. The solution to this problem is going to be worse than the crime.

After Hannah left, I lay on my bed and brooded for a while. Then I got up to read another stack of submissions for <u>The Daisy</u>. The writing took my mind off thieves and missing property. And this time I didn't get upset reading the submissions. The bad pieces didn't annoy me, and the good ones didn't discourage me.

Thanks, mysterious thief. You've done at least one positive thing, even though you didn't mean to.

Or am I just getting used to being an editor?

Chapter 10

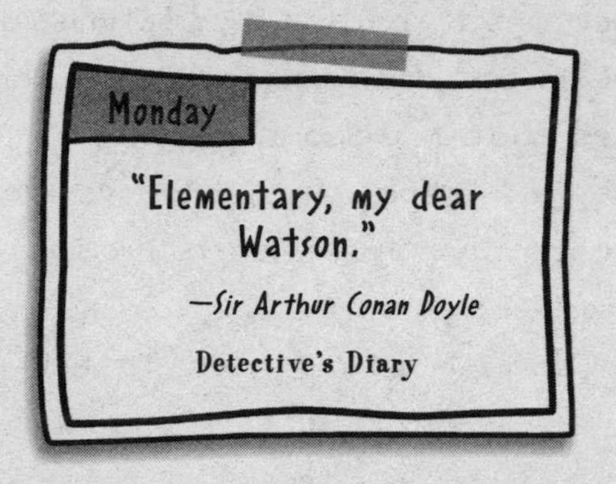

Elementary is the word.

Former Lancaster Elementary students are losing things faster than a tree loses its leaves in the fall.

Now Jonathan's magnifying glass has disappeared. Crystal is missing a plum-colored lipstick. Casey "misplaced" an autographed baseball.

Hannah thinks we are hot on the trail of the thief, but I am utterly stumped.

Who's next?

Can we trust anyone anymore?

It's not safe to bring a journal to school. I've hidden it in a secure place in my room. My journal is now officially in exile.

When I need to write in school, I'll use scraps of paper or napkins or the backs of old math tests, then copy everything into my journal each night.

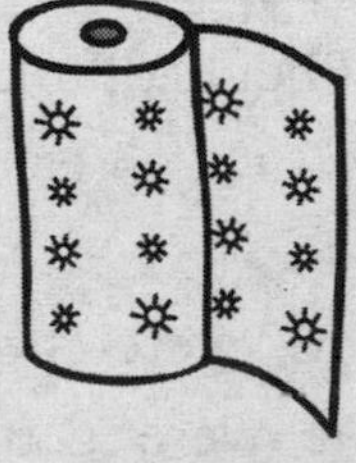

No more space left on this paper towel. So I'll end here and head to gym class.

The school nurse handed Abby an ice pack wrapped in a washcloth. "Here, dear," she said. "It'll help take the pain away."

Abby pressed the ice pack to her aching forehead.

"I don't know why they call it softball," she groaned. "There's *nothing* soft about it."

"Yes, that's quite a bruise," the nurse said cheerfully. "And it's the third gym class injury I've seen this morning. Everything always happens in clusters. Funny how that works. So, someone threw the ball at your head?"

"Not deliberately," Abby said. "I was looking the other way. I didn't even see it coming."

She had been thinking, as usual, about the Lancaster Elementary thief.

The nurse clucked her tongue. "Any nausea? Shooting pains? Dizziness?"

"I feel a little dizzy," Abby said.

"Why don't you lie down for a few minutes?" The nurse pointed to a small bed behind a screen.

"Okay, thanks." Abby stretched out on the cot. Now it was easier to hold the ice pack against her head.

Kids were coming in and out of the nurse's office. Some were getting medication, while others complained of headaches, or were having asthma attacks.

Abby had never known what a busy place the nurse's office was. Maybe doing the Health News for the school newspaper wouldn't have been so bad, after all.

In spite of all the noise, her eyes closed. And then she dozed off. A moment later, she started awake.

"I was feeling just a teensy bit nauseous," a familiar voice chirped. "And then the room started spinning around me. I feel like a hamster on a wheel."

Through an opening in the screen, Abby could see Bethany at the nurse's desk. Her face was pale. She was clutching her stomach.

Next to her, Brianna tapped her foot impatiently.

"Do you feel feverish?" the nurse asked.

Bethany shook her head. She set her pink backpack down in front of the desk. "I just feel a teensy bit nauseous," she repeated.

"This better not be contagious," Brianna said. "I have a performance at the City Theater tomorrow night."

"Brianna, you're the best," Bethany croaked loyally. "Thanks for coming here with me. Yay, Brianna."

"Can I leave now?" Brianna demanded.

The nurse took out a thermometer and shook it. "Open your mouth," she said to Bethany. "There's a nasty stomach virus going around."

Brianna backed out of the room. "I'm out of here," she said, practically bumping into Natalie, who was on her way in.

Uh-oh, thought Abby. Brianna, Bethany, and Natalie in the same place at the same time. Trouble.

"*Excuse* me!" Brianna huffed.

"Watch where you're going," Natalie snapped. She approached the nurse's desk and held out some papers. "I have the forms filled out for my physical."

The nurse took the thermometer from Bethany's mouth. "Just a minute," she said to Natalie. "I'll be right with you."

"Sick?" Natalie said to Bethany.

Bethany nodded.

"That stinks," Natalie said sympathetically.

"I was supposed to volunteer at the animal shelter today after school," Bethany said plaintively.

"You have a fever of 101," the nurse announced. "I'm calling your parents. Is one of them at home?"

Bethany suddenly turned even paler. "I think . . . I think . . . I think I'm going to throw up," she said.

"Right this way, dear." The nurse hustled Bethany toward the bathroom. The door closed behind them.

For a moment, the nurse's office was silent. Natalie stared out the window, looking bored. She didn't see Abby lying behind the screen and Abby didn't call out to her. Her head was still throbbing. She held the ice pack to the bruise and hoped that Natalie and Bethany would become close friends again.

Abby closed her eyes. From the bathroom, she

heard the nurse's kind murmur and the sound of water running.

When she opened her eyes again, Natalie was leaning over Bethany's backpack. As Abby watched in horror, Natalie unzipped one of the compartments, took out a small leather coin purse in the shape of a cow, and slipped it silently into her own backpack.

Then she placed her papers on the nurse's desk and sauntered out of the room.

Chapter 11

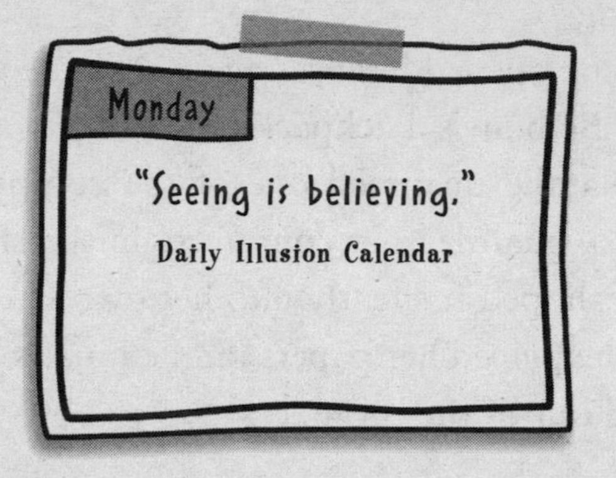

Even though I saw it, I still don't believe it.

Natalie is the thief?

<u>Natalie?</u>

<u>NATALIE</u>?

The Natalie I know wouldn't steal from her friends or her ex-friends. This isn't like her at all.

Besides, Natalie has everything she needs. Doesn't she?

Maybe she's just temporarily mad at Brianna and Bethany? Maybe she's NOT the one who stole from me, Hannah, Mason, Casey, Jonathan, and Crystal?

I wish this was true.

This is worse than being hit in the head with a softball. This is worse than having my pen stolen. This is worse than worrying about having my journal stolen. This is worse than <u>anything</u>.

As she left English class, Abby put her hand to the bump on her forehead. The nurse had covered it with a bandage and told her to come back for ice whenever she needed it.

"When you get home, have your parents give you some ibuprofen," she instructed. "We can't give you medicine in school without a signed authorization."

"That's all right," Abby said. "It doesn't hurt too much."

Her head was barely bothering her anymore, but she felt like every other part of herself was in pain.

Was there a medicine that would take away the hurt of discovering that Natalie was a thief? And that she was stealing from her closest friends?

As Abby headed down the hallway to her science class, she passed Brianna and one of her admirers.

"And Bethany's face looked *green*!" Brianna exclaimed. "She almost fainted, but I caught her and practically carried her to the nurse's office. The nurse said that I had saved her from total collapse."

"When did she say *that*?" Abby muttered under her breath. "I was there the whole time."

Brianna continued, "Heroism is a daily event for someone like me. . . ." She broke off in mid-brag. "Natalie!"

Abby stiffened. She held her breath as Natalie glided toward Brianna. Natalie's expression was untroubled and calm.

"How's Bethany?" Brianna asked. "Did you see her?"

Natalie shrugged. "I just dropped off some papers for the nurse," she said. "I was only in the office for thirty seconds."

No, that was a lie, Abby thought. Natalie had

waited at the desk. She had seen Bethany go into the bathroom with the nurse.

And she had stayed long enough to steal a change purse from Bethany's backpack.

"I have a performance at the City Theater tomorrow night," Brianna announced to anyone who was listening. "That stomach virus better stay away."

Natalie looked bored. She walked away.

Suddenly Abby was furious. She ran after Natalie, even though her science class was in the opposite direction. She'd make up an excuse for being late or just take the teacher's scolding.

As she wove in and out of the stream of students, she wondered what she'd do if Natalie actually stole something right in front of her. Would she yell, "Stop! Thief!"?

Of course not. She couldn't do that to a friend. But she couldn't just stand by and watch Natalie steal, could she?

What did you say to a friend who was doing something wrong? Who had stolen from *you*?

Natalie stopped, bent over a water fountain, and took a drink. She straightened and adjusted her backpack. Suddenly she whirled around and faced Abby.

"Abby. I thought that was you. . . ." She stopped. "What happened to your forehead?"

"Softball accident," Abby said. Her pulse raced. She wasn't ready for this. She hoped Natalie wouldn't guess that she'd been in the nurse's office that morning.

"Are you on your way to science?"

"Uh, yeah." Too late, she remembered that Natalie used to be in that class with her.

"You're heading in the wrong direction," Natalie pointed out.

"I was following you," Abby blurted, regretting the words before they were out of her mouth.

Natalie looked annoyed. "You were following me?"

Now what did she say? *I saw you stealing in the nurse's office.* Or, *I know you're the thief, please stop*. Or, *Why are you doing this, Natalie?* Or even, *I want my earrings returned*, now.

But no words came to her.

Desperately, Abby glanced around the hallway. Kids were disappearing through doorways, laughing and pushing each other.

A boy waved to her. It was Lucas. Abby waved

back. Seeing him gave her an idea. She turned to Natalie.

"Would you like to submit something to the next issue of *The Daisy*?"

"I don't write," Natalie said.

Abby rushed on. "But we're looking for photography, too. Our theme is beginnings. The Jazz Tones are a new musical ensemble. Why don't you take some pictures and send them to us?"

Natalie shook her head. "No, not now. I can't. Maybe another time."

"Sure. I understand. Keep us in mind."

As she headed back toward the other wing of the building, Abby felt limp with relief. *That was close!* She had almost blurted something out, something that she wasn't ready to say yet.

But she knew that she had only postponed the painful confrontation. She was going to have to speak to Natalie sooner or later.

Chapter 12

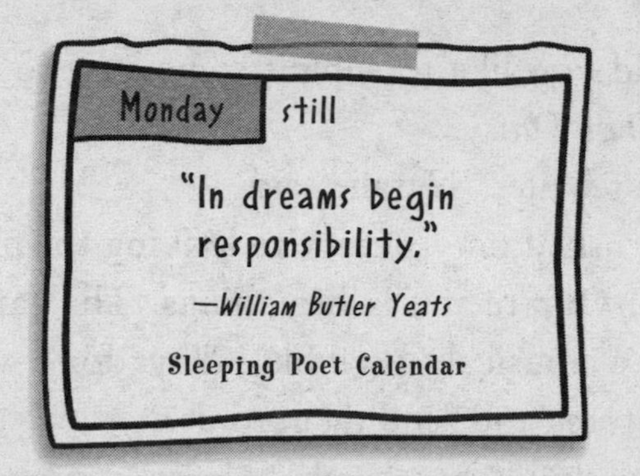

This isn't a dream. I wish it were.

I might be the only person in Susan B. Anthony Middle School who knows that Natalie is the thief.

And I feel SO responsible.

Everyone is upset about their missing things.

Does Simon know what's going on? Is she stealing from him, too?

Sooner or later, all of Natalie's friends are going to feel betrayed, confused, upset, and angry, just like I do. People are going to turn against her when they find out.

I'm also scared for Natalie. Doesn't she realize what's going to happen?

If she doesn't stop soon, she'll get caught. She might be suspended. The principal might call her parents. Someone might even call the police!

I have to do something. But I don't know what.

"Abby! Wait up!" Simon was loping toward her with a long stride. His brown hair fell over his forehead into his eyes. He wore jeans and a dark green T-shirt.

It was Monday after school; Abby was on her way home. She was looking forward to writing in her journal in the quiet privacy of her room. Today had been full of excitement, almost all of the wrong kind.

"Do you have a minute? I need to speak to you. Alone."

Alone? With Simon? Her heart began to pound madly. What for?

Maybe, like Natalie, he was upset that she had left the Jazz Tones. If Abby explained about being an editor on *The Daisy*, would he understand?

"It won't take long," he said. "I promise. It's kind of important."

"Um, sure." Abby wondered if David's new assistant was working out. She hoped Simon wasn't going to ask her to rejoin the Jazz Tones.

Then she had a sudden wild thought that he was going to confess a crush. But why would he confide in *her*?

Simon stared at her bandaged forehead. "What happened to you?"

"I had a close encounter with a softball."

"Poor softball," he teased, falling into step beside her.

"The softball survived," Abby said. She tried to sound nonchalant. "So what's up?"

Simon looked upset. "It's Natalie."

Heat rushed into Abby's face. She felt sick to her stomach. "Natalie," she repeated in a whisper. "What's wrong?"

He frowned. "You're good friends. Didn't she tell you?"

"She hasn't told me anything," Abby said. "She's not the confiding type."

"No, she isn't," he agreed. "I only found out by accident."

Abby drew in her breath sharply. So Simon knew, too.

"Same here," she said. "I discovered it today in the nurse's office. But Natalie doesn't know that I know."

For a moment, neither of them said anything.

Simon broke the silence. "Tell me what you heard in the nurse's office. I want to know what he's done now."

"He? You mean she, right?"

"I mean *he*," Simon said. "Nicholas. We're talking about her brother, aren't we?"

She shook her head. "*I'm* talking about Natalie."

Simon thought for a moment. Then he said, "I have to tell you a secret. Do you promise not to tell anyone?"

Abby nodded. Were she and Simon really having this conversation? She couldn't quite believe it.

"Natalie's brother, Nicholas, got suspended from school," Simon said.

"He did?" Abby cried. "What for?"

"I don't know. But it must have been something really bad. . . ."

"Oh," Abby said slowly. This explained a few things. Or at least made them easier to understand.

"It's really hard on Natalie," Simon said. "She's not herself lately."

"I've noticed that." Abby had thought Natalie's bad moods were because of Bethany. But now there was her brother, too.

"What happened in the nurse's office?" Simon asked again.

Abby hesitated. She really ought to talk to Hannah first. But Hannah wasn't here; Simon was. And he knew Natalie much better than Hannah did.

Instead of answering, she said, "Why aren't you at rehearsal today?"

"The Jazz Tones got canceled. David has the stomach flu," he said. "He blames it on working in a middle school."

"Sounds like David," Abby said drily. It still hurt to think about the way he had dismissed her.

"David is demanding," Simon admitted. "Okay, he's difficult. But it's worth it. We're turning into a really great band."

He suddenly grabbed Abby's hand. "Please tell me about the nurse's office. I'm worried about Natalie. That's why I wanted to talk to you. I thought you'd know what to do."

Abby melted. Simon was holding her *hand*. He was asking for help. And he was concerned about Natalie.

He was Natalie's friend, too. He cared about her. How could she *not* tell him?

"Simon," she said, "have you heard about the Lancaster Elementary thief?"

He frowned. "I've heard a few kids mention him."

"It's not a him, it's a her."

"So?"

"It's Natalie."

"Natalie?" Simon repeated in shock.

"Natalie," Abby said.

Simon looked dazed. "You're *sure* it's her?"

"Sure," Abby said firmly. "Today in the nurse's office, I saw her take a leather coin purse from Bethany's backpack. It was shaped like a cow," she added.

Simon pulled a tissue from his pocket and wiped his forehead. "This is crazy," he said. "I can't believe she'd do something like this."

"Me, either."

"What do we do?" For the first time since she had met him, Simon seemed at a loss. "Shouldn't we go to the guidance counselor? Or to the principal?"

These were the same words Abby had said to Hannah only a short time ago. But now she found herself arguing against them.

"We'd get Natalie in a lot of trouble. She might get suspended, like her brother."

"You're right. Her parents would be furious," Simon said. "They're very strict. Do you think we should talk to her?"

"Natalie is so proud. I wonder if she'll listen to us."

He sighed deeply.

"Does it matter?" Abby said suddenly. "Maybe we should try, anyway."

Simon nodded in agreement. "All right. When?"

"Now?" Abby couldn't believe she was doing this.

"Let's meet in an hour," Simon proposed. "Together we'll pay a surprise visit to Natalie."

He smiled his dazzling smile. And then he did something that Abby *really* couldn't believe. He put his arm around her and hugged her.

Chapter 13

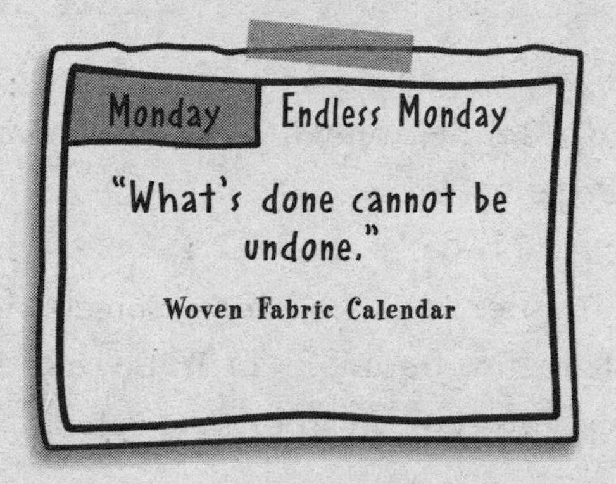

Things That Can't Be Undone:

1. Natalie's stealing
2. The shared secrets that Simon and I told each other
3. Simon's hand-squeeze and hug!!

I still can't believe it!

It all seems unreal. Did Simon really hold my hand and hug me? Did I really see Natalie steal today? Are Simon and I actually going to talk to her about it?

Are we out of our minds?

And should I tell Hannah or not?

Do Tell:

If I do tell Hannah, I won't ever be able to take it back.

What if she says or does something that gets Natalie in trouble? It'll be my fault for telling Hannah in the first place.

Don't Tell:

If I don't tell Hannah about Natalie, she might never forgive me.

When Hannah finds out that I discovered the thief and didn't tell her, she might be hurt and angry. She might also be upset that I didn't invite her to join Simon and me.

But I didn't exclude Hannah on purpose. I didn't WANT to find the thief. And Simon chased after me and told me his secret first.

I have to admit it's exciting to share a

secret with Simon. But I can't think about that now.

I can't even worry about Hannah. I have a very serious problem to solve. Like, what are Simon and I going to say to Natalie?

<u>What We Are Going to Say to Natalie</u>:

1. "We know you're the thief, so stop doing it."

2. "Please return everyone's things before you get into trouble."

3. "Why are you doing this, Natalie? Don't you realize how dangerous it is?"

4. "We're your friends. You can trust us. We want to help you."

Will these words reach her?

Will she listen?

Will she return Hannah's bracelet and my silver earrings?

Will she stop stealing?

Or will Simon and I have to turn her in?

Chapter 14

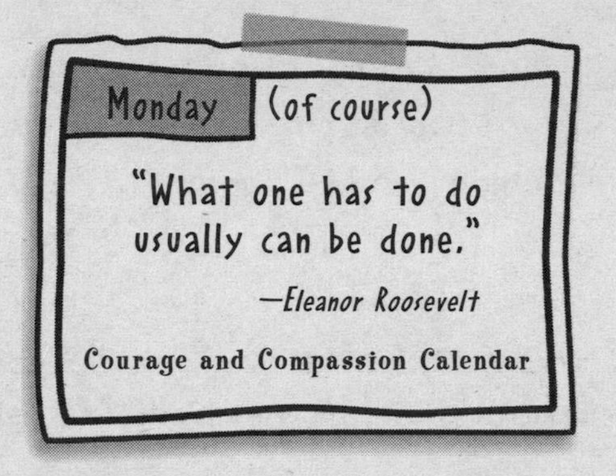

This has to be done. It must be done. It better be done. It can be done. We are going to do it!

Three Wishes:

1. To have the courage to talk to Natalie
2. To find exactly the right words to say to her
3. To not make a worse mess than this already is

Three More Wishes:

1. To not embarrass myself in front of Simon

2. That Simon will like me more than ever

3. For Simon to hug me again!!!

Chapter 15

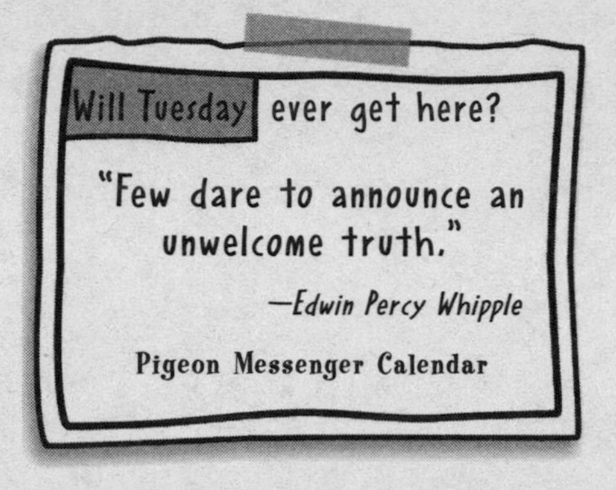

Yes, and I know why. It's **really** scary.

Simon and I will dare to announce an unwelcome truth to Natalie. We will tell her all that we know, whether she likes it or not.

And now it's really time to go!

Simon looked calm and cool and unafraid as he and Abby waited on Natalie's doorstep for someone to answer the bell.

Abby *hoped* she looked cool and calm and unafraid. She didn't feel any of those things. She wanted to run away. If Simon hadn't been standing at her side, she would have done it.

Simon pushed the doorbell a second time. "She should be home," he said. "She was going to practice her clarinet."

Abby pressed her ear to the door. "I can't hear anything."

At that moment, the door swung open. Abby lost her balance and stumbled into the front hallway.

She grabbed the door frame to steady herself. It had only been three minutes since they arrived at Natalie's house and she had already embarrassed herself. That had to be some sort of world record.

"Hello?" It was Natalie's mother. She looked tired and her eyes had dark circles under them. She didn't seem to recognize Abby, although Abby had been to her house many times. "Can I help you?"

"Um. Hi! Is Natalie home?" Abby said, trying to regain her poise as well as her footing.

"We're here to see her," Simon added unnecessarily.

Natalie's mother went to the bottom of the stairs, yelled, "Natalie! For you!" then disappeared into the house.

Abby looked at Simon. "That was weird," she whispered.

"Yeah," Simon agreed. He seemed uncomfortable now, too.

Natalie came down the stairs. She was wearing black jeans and a black top. Her face was pale and her mouth was tense.

"What do you want?" she said in an unfriendly voice.

Abby glanced at Simon. Simon glanced at Abby.

"Can we talk?" Abby said.

Natalie shrugged. "Go ahead."

"Not here. We want to talk to you in private," Simon said.

A shadow crossed Natalie's face — or did Abby imagine it?

"This isn't a good time," she said. "I'm not supposed to have any visitors in the house right now."

"Not even for fifteen minutes?" Abby had somehow imagined the three of them in Natalie's room, having, in her mother's words, "a calm, civilized discussion."

If she and Simon had to leave now, Abby didn't know if she'd have the courage to come back a second time.

"Can we go talk in your backyard?" Simon suggested.

"All right," Natalie said sullenly.

She slipped on some sandals and shut the front door behind them. Then she led them into the yard.

A small, empty fountain stood in the middle of the yard, and a high wooden fence completely surrounded it.

"How about over there?" Simon said, pointing to some chairs under a walnut tree some distance from the house.

"That looks good," Abby said.

Natalie said nothing.

They sat down. There was an awkward silence.

Natalie stared at Abby as if challenging her to say something.

"Um, well, uh . . ." Abby began. All the eloquent words that she had rehearsed so carefully on the way over here had vanished.

Simon coughed and shifted in his chair. If anything, he seemed even more ill at ease than Abby.

"I have practicing to do," Natalie said in an aloof tone. "And my parents expect me to help with dinner."

"Natalie . . ." Simon and Abby blurted at the same time. They looked at each other and reddened.

"Uh, Natalie," Simon tried again.

"This is about . . ." Abby tried.

Natalie lifted an eyebrow.

"I saw you in the nurse's office today," Abby blurted out. "I saw what you did." She couldn't quite bring herself to say the words.

Natalie turned even paler but remained motionless.

"We *know*," Simon said awkwardly. "We know what's going on."

"So?" Natalie said.

"So?" Abby repeated. She had expected denial, not cool defiance. "What if a teacher sees you? What if you get thrown out of school?"

"I don't care," Natalie said stonily.

"It's theft, you know. You can go to jail."

"Everyone knows your mother is a lawyer, Abby," Natalie said. "You don't have to rub it in."

Abby's eyes flashed, but she didn't reply.

"We're worried about you, Natalie," Simon said in a conciliatory tone.

"Yes," Abby seconded him. "We don't want you to get in trouble."

"That's so *nice* of you," Natalie sneered. "Now that you've been so kind and good, why don't you go home?"

"Why are you so bitter and nasty?" Abby burst out. "We're your friends!"

Natalie stood up and folded her arms across her chest.

"You *have* to stop stealing things," Simon said. "Otherwise you're going to get in trouble like your brother."

"Will you leave now?" Natalie's eyes glittered with fury and tears.

Abby stood up. "We're not going home until you give back all the things that you've stolen!" she cried. "And until you promise *never* to do it again!"

Simon nodded in agreement.

Natalie stared at them in disbelief. Then she turned and ran into the house, slamming the door behind her.

"Did I go too far?" Abby asked in a low voice. "Was I too tough?"

Simon shook his head.

"Should we leave?"

"No," he said.

"What if she sends her mother to throw us out?"

"So we'll get thrown out."

Neither of them said another word.

The back door opened with a bang. Natalie reappeared, carrying a bag. She walked over to where Abby and Simon were waiting and threw it down on the grass in front of them.

"Good riddance," she said bitterly.

"Do you promise not to *ever* do it . . ." Simon began.

"Spare me the lecture!" Natalie spat. Without another word, she stalked back into the house.

"We did it," Simon said. With a deep sigh, he picked up the bag. "Let's get out of here before she changes her mind."

Chapter 16

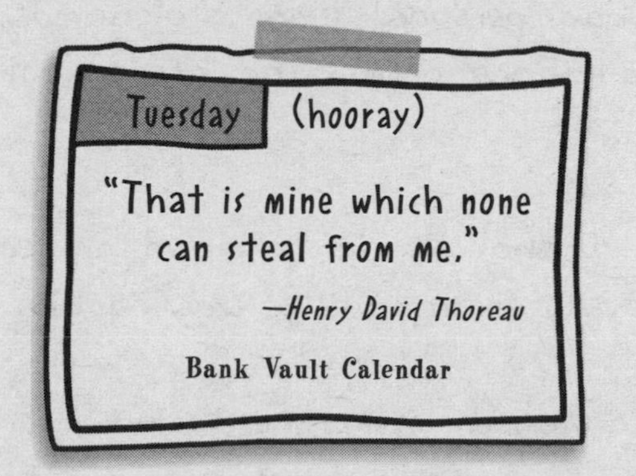

Simon and I put all the stolen things in a small box with a typed list of what belonged to who. I didn't take my earrings out. I didn't want to seem different than anyone else. We sealed the box tightly and brought it to school early this morning hidden inside Simon's backpack.

Simon gave it to one of the guidance counselors. I'm not sure how he explained it, but he did.

This morning there was an announcement over the PA system.

"Any sixth-graders who have recently lost or had personal items stolen may come to the guidance office and identify their property."

When I showed up to claim my earrings, Mason was triumphantly waving his science pencil.

Bethany cried when she found her hamster key chain and her change purse. Her money was still inside.

"Mine!" Brianna cried as she pulled her Me magazine and Tiffany Crystal CD from the box. She deposited them in the white leather backpack and flounced out of the guidance office.

Zach picked up his electronic game player and kissed it right in front of everyone!

Hannah took her bracelet. Her eyes met mine. I shrugged, and carefully put on my earrings.

All day the sixth grade was buzzing. Who stole the items? Why were they returned? Why did they reappear in the guidance office this morning?

It was interesting to hear everyone's theories.

At first Mason thought it was a conspiracy, but then he decided that the "Lancaster Elementary Thief Mystery" will turn up as an entry in the Science Fair next spring. He claims that it's a study of kids' responses to losing personal property and that we can expect an exhibit with photographs and flowcharts and scientific data.

Bethany says that it really WAS a thief and that he or she had an attack of conscience. She's sure that they couldn't sleep at night and _had_ to return the stolen items.

"No one steals from ME," Brianna announced. "I have cousins on the police force. They were outraged by my losses and put top undercover detectives on the case. You see how quickly they cracked it."

Hannah kept saying that she was on the verge of figuring everything out, and she wished she knew what had happened.

I didn't say much of anything.

I didn't see Simon for the rest of the day.

I didn't see Natalie at all.

"Abby, would you do me a favor?" Olivia Hayes put her hand on her daughter's shoulder. "I have some last-minute errands to run. Will you pick up a few items for me at the drugstore?"

"Sure, Mom," Abby said.

It was late Saturday morning. Abby and her mother were at the mall, buying new clothes. Abby had gotten several cute T-shirts and some wide-legged pants. She had also talked her mother into buying her a new purple bathrobe with orange cats on it.

Now they had almost everything on their list. Only a few final errands remained.

"Thanks, honey," Abby's mother said. "That'll help us get out of here faster. You know how much I *adore* malls and shopping." Olivia made a face. She didn't like shopping trips at all. They were a waste of time in her busy life.

"I love malls!" Abby said. Automatically, she touched her ears and the silver earrings that Eva had given her. She had gotten her ears pierced in this very mall. She had done it secretly, with her friends. Her parents hadn't been happy, but she had been allowed to keep the earrings.

If she hadn't been allowed to pierce her ears, she wondered, what would Natalie have stolen from her? Her purple pen? Or her journal?

Olivia opened her purse and gave Abby some money and a shopping list. "I'll meet you in front of the department store in half an hour," she said.

"Can I keep the change?" Abby said hopefully, looking at the pile of five- and ten-dollar bills that her mother had just handed her.

"Good try, Abby," her mother said, amused. "You got your allowance this morning. I think that's enough."

Abby filled a shopping basket with toothpaste, shampoo, conditioner, cough drops, bandages, and callus remover. Then she went to the deodorant aisle.

Deodorant. Ugh. Why did her mother have to put *that* on the list? It was really embarrassing.

"Ultra Pink?" she muttered. "Extra sensitive, unscented? Where *is* it?"

Suddenly she saw it. She reached out her hand to pluck it off the shelf.

"Abby?" a boy's voice said.

Her hand dropped. Abby jumped away from the deodorant display, and pretended to be studying a row of hair spray cans with shiny lettering.

"Lucas," Abby said in dismay. She hoped he hadn't seen her reaching for the deodorant.

Lucas was carrying a package of diapers. "You don't use that hair spray stuff on your hair, do you?" he asked critically. "It's really bad for the environment. And it's not good for you, either."

"I'm doing errands for my mother," Abby informed him with as much dignity as she could muster. "You don't use *those*, do you?" She pointed to the diapers.

Lucas just grinned. Why were boys embarrassment-proof?

"They're for my baby brother. Half-brother," he said. "My father got remarried last year."

"Oh," Abby said. She wondered what it was like to have a new mother and a new brother just like that.

"My baby brother goes through piles of these things." Lucas hoisted the diapers on his shoulder. "I tried to convince Claire, my stepmother, to use a diaper service, but she won't."

"Oh," Abby said again. Lucas was capable of talking about *anything*. She just hoped he wouldn't start talking about the embarrassing products on display all around them.

"I have an idea for the literary journal," he said instead.

Abby almost sighed with relief. "Tell me," she said.

"Remember how I wanted to write a story about the Lancaster Elementary thief?" Lucas said. "You know, a kind of whodunit."

Abby sighed. She wished he had forgotten all about it. "It doesn't fit with our beginnings theme," she warned him. She didn't want him poking around and maybe finding out about Natalie. Lucas would never keep quiet.

"What about a crime theme for the next issue?"

"A *crime* issue? For middle school?"

Lucas gestured impatiently. "Never mind the theme! What do you think of the *idea*?"

"Um, it's okay. But isn't the story too close to real life?"

"The best fiction gets written from life," Lucas insisted.

"No, it doesn't," Abby retorted. "Imagination has a *lot* more to do with it."

"But I'm planning to use my imagination," Lucas said. "I've already figured out that the thief is a poor boy who has nothing of his own. Only why would he return the stuff? Maybe he's afraid of being caught."

"A poor boy?" Abby repeated. "I like that. Maybe he's in trouble already and doesn't want to make things worse."

"Awesome," Lucas said. "Will you read it for me? When I'm done, I mean. I haven't started yet."

"Sure," Abby said. "Why not?"

"Thank you, fellow editor." Lucas made a mock bow. Then he balanced the diapers under his arm and headed for the checkout line.

As soon as Lucas was out of sight, Abby grabbed the Ultra Pink and hid it at the bottom of the basket. She hurried into the next aisle to buy some dental floss that she had forgotten, and then got into line at the cash register.

"Thank you for shopping at Peerless Price-saving

Prescriptions," the clerk said. She put all of Abby's purchases into a large plastic bag and stapled it shut. "Have a nice day."

Abby pocketed the change and headed toward the department store to meet her mother. She was right on time. But her mother wasn't there yet.

Abby leaned against the display window. Another girl was waiting, too.

She was standing a few feet away. Her arms were laden with packages. She was staring into the distance. She didn't seem to notice Abby.

Then she turned and saw her.

For a moment, neither of them said anything.

"Hi, Natalie," Abby finally said.

"Hello," Natalie returned.

"Shopping?" Abby asked awkwardly.

Natalie nodded.

"I'm waiting for my mother. You, too?"

"My aunt." Natalie shifted her position.

Abby took a deep breath. "What did you buy?"

"Stuff."

"Me, too," Abby said. "Stuff."

"There's my aunt," Natalie said, pointing to a plump woman staring intently at a display of bedspreads.

"I hope everything's okay," Abby said hesitantly. "Your brother and . . ."

Natalie looked away.

She should have kept her mouth shut, Abby thought. The stolen things had been returned and there had been no more thefts. Natalie had kept her word. Wasn't that enough?

But suddenly Natalie mumbled, "Thanks for not saying anything to anyone."

"Simon and I are keeping your secret." Abby hadn't told Hannah or anyone else. And no one knew what she and Simon had done.

Abby and Simon had gone through something important together. They had a special bond now. The secret tied them together.

"It's safe with us," she reassured Natalie.

"Well, thanks," Natalie said again. Her eyes were bright. "And I'm sorry. . . ." She broke off. Her aunt was approaching. "I have to go now. Good-bye."

"Good-bye," Abby said. She watched Natalie walk away.

My mother showed up a few minutes after Natalie left. She treated me to a chocolate pretzel and then we went home. Sophia is coming over in half an hour. I have just enough time to write down some thoughts.

Who Could Have Imagined?

(A very odd list, by Abby Hayes)

1. That Natalie would steal

2. That I would discover it

3. That Simon would come to me for advice

4. That I'd team up with Simon

5. That Simon and I would take care of things together

6. That Simon actually hugged me!!!! (I'm still in shock.)

7. That we became much closer, even though I quit the Jazz Tones

8. That I didn't share an important secret with Hannah

9. That I don't regret it, this time

10. That I'm thinking of asking Lucas's opinion about a story I wrote (Maybe.)

11. That Natalie said thank you and practically apologized!!!!???

12. That she didn't get in trouble and things turned out okay

13. That she's not even mad at me????

14. That I'd have so many strange and unexpected events to write about!

There's the doorbell. It must be Sophia. I wonder what's going to happen next?